I've been reading and enjoying Joe Young's microfiction for years now. He can do more in 50 words than any writer I know. The tiny stories in Easter Rabbit are complete and whole, with language that surprises and never grows stale.

Mary Miller, author of *Big World*

What's disarming is how effective these stories are in *Easter Rabbit*. You expect something so terse to feel incomplete, a mere piece of some greater whole, but the stories, moments, relationships, and feelings in these 100 pages end up saying all they need to in an artfully precise use of language.

Baltimore *City Paper*

These stories tick along with such sentences until the camera starts to melt: the world suddenly understood not through mimetic language but through the imposition of imagination. Conversations invent machines, a spider bite invents a vision of God ... Their job is to permute our circumstances and our language until they've uncovered new ways to make our world mysterious again.

Mike Young, *NOÖ Journal*

It's tempting to compare Joseph's marvelous collection of microfictions to many things, miniature portraits, maybe, or model ships inside bottles, or flashes of lives glimpsed through windows in the night. But when writing is as honest and true as this, it seems wrong to call it anything but what it is: very very short, very very good stories, each one grasping at "starlight . . . out of reach" with "small and smaller tries."

Pasha Malla, author of *The Withdrawal Method*

Those who liked their fiction well-defined or gobbled up and forgotten after a single reading, will find *Easter Rabbit* vexing. But in its open-ended form, in its prism-like prose, this is one book that the reader can return to again and again to see new meanings. In that sense, I believe the book is worth far more than its price.

David Woodruff, *The Short Review*

The bottom line is that Young takes situations that seem, mostly, fairly mundane, and breathes meaning into them. A man sees a black rat running through the leaves and this becomes a beautiful moment.

CL Bledsoe, *Ghoti Magazine*

With their directness and precision, their attention to what Ezra Pound would call "luminous details," Joseph Young's microfictions might be mistaken for Imagist poems, but with their shift away from showing "things" as "things" toward "things" as something else, or, rather, toward portraying both the "thingness" of the thing and of some different "thing," his miniatures suggest something altogether different.

John Madera, *New Pages*

These are not stories in the traditional sense and I can't really compare this writing to any other, which is a very good thing. I feel both smarter and dumber reading Joseph Young's work, but ultimately I feel … nourished. Because he brings to writing what I go to writing for and that is the beauty and depth of a true artist.

Kathy Fish, *JMWW*

The relationship between text and reader becomes transactional, how much are we willing to give and how much do we want to take. The small texts draw us in and the white space requires us to go beyond the page, beyond the comfort of the words and to our own black box.

Megan Lavelle, *BMoreArt*

Something will sneak up on you [in these stories], something long forgotten, the back of your head will fall out and you will remember

the time you took that big breath and really felt the heaviness of all your surroundings.
    David Peak, *Ghost Factory*

Easter Rabbit takes words and makes them mean more, makes them hit us harder, makes us see better how language functions in short breaths, in gasps, in tight fists.
    JA Tyler, *Rumble*

This is an IMPORTANT book. Some reviewer predicted early in Richard Brautigan's career that he was creating a new genre, that one day we'd read novels, poems, short stories, and 'brautigans.' He was right, even if common parlance has yet to catch up. Enter the new mode of writing: 'joe-youngs.'
    John Dermot Woods, *Big Other*

Young's microfictions function like emergency life rafts in that he gets this ostensibly small bit of material into your head and then pulls the cord and something huge unfolds.
    Josh Maday, *htmlgiant*

Filled with pleasure and surprise, Easter Rabbit is a series of haunting whispers that resonate. With a voice of stunning curiosity, Joe Young's microfiction is graceful and unique, a satisfying, tasteful indulgence.
    Kim Chinquee, author of *Pretty*

Joe Young's lovely little fictions present objects and parts, voices guiding voices, striking images in solid prose. A city of familiar scenes rises around the reader, who may be surprised to find how quickly they attach and draw her near. These are puzzles best devoured slowly.
    Amelia Gray, author of *Museum of the Weird*

EASTER RABBIT
BY JOSEPH YOUNG

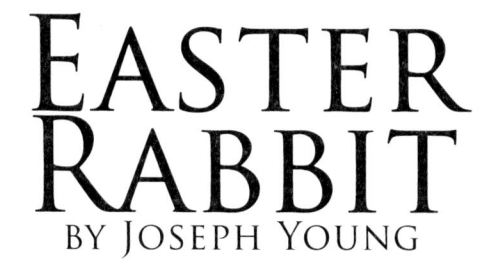

Publishing Genius
Baltimore, 2009

Published by Publishing Genius
Baltimore, MD 2009
Copyright © Joseph Young
Cover painting by Christine Sajecki

Easter Rabbit first published by Publishing Genius Press in 2009
ISBN 10: 0-9820813-4-0
ISBN 13: 978-0-9820813-4-1

The following stories appeared in *FRiGG Magazine*: Occupation; Interruption; Exegesis; Pike; &1/4; Valentine; Biography; Cradle; Menlo Park; Oglala; Lease; Manifest. The following stories appeared in *Lamination Colony*: Constant Math; On Not To See A Bird; Incorporated. The following stories appeared in *Grey Sparrow Journal*: Fault; Grand; East-Eden; 80; At Last. The following stories appeared in *Caketrain*: Argot; Epistemology; Absorbance. The story Cardinal appeared in *wigleaf*. The story Another Thing appears with the permission of Adam Robinson. The story Lily appears in *Keyhole*. The original broadside of God Not Otherwise appeared as *This PDF Chapbook #6* from Publishing Genius. Selected stories from Deep Falls appeared in *JMWW*. Deep Falls was a collaborative art project and show with encaustic painter Christine Sajecki; the show appeared at Antreasian Gallery, Baltimore, February 2008. The story Epistemology appears in the film *60 Writers / 60 Places* from Little Burn Films.

Contents

Easter Rabbit　1
Stories Around People　61
More from Stories Around People　65
Deep Falls　67
God Not Otherwise　89

EASTER RABBIT

SINE

A white line, across the cement, under the park, through the door, faint and hardly there, to its red center.

Marie Celeste

The cup moons beneath her eyes were in decline. *You know the tsunami?* she said. *Except that all of it was ping-pong balls.* It was evening again already, pushed fingernails against the palm.

We Need Supper

They tried force, one then another. I work, said one. Sex, joked a second. A certain movie, the third. The women at the other tables were like starlight, blue and keen, out of reach. The space among them, over the hot sauce and napkin pile, was the only true thing. Lonely, it said and, Why do we want? The men had no choice but to confront their silverware, the jabbing at and eating of small, masked admission. The evening wore on. Perhaps there was time. They needed some way out, through the jaws of their coffee cups or the last lowering of hands.

Oglala

If I were to die ... she said.

She left it at that, measuring the table with her arm, ribs to fingertip. He considered that future: like tall grass never stopping waving.

Constant Math

Things he decided: ice was always bitter, time will append like cooking oil, he'd only been wrong once. That was as a boy. There was a girl, her small ear, purple in the mulberry tree.

Some Things Stand For Things

The wind clung to him, his arms trailing strings of it as it blew. Across the narrow meadow was a man, one eye blackened out, the other rolling. The man gestured to him to come, that there was an opening in the hill. I can't, he shouted. It's too far. The man shook himself and spat. He'd known the type, these boys who would smother in the sun before taking a hand.

LILY

The snake tasted the air. Among the cold shale, high desert night, were spots of heat, a rat, a small bird. The snake smelled them, alone, not alone, the bandaged feet of birth.

Girl

The tadpoles flipped on the brown mud bottom. She dipped one out and held it near, seeing it in her belly, shaping arms and feet and a small, blond head. She set it back and stood, breasts out, arms up. The ducks in the weed, eyes hard like hungry boys, waited for bread. She would call, I hate you, or, I love you, and the ducks would scatter. She would do neither. The mud sucked her shoes, the minnows showed their silver stomachs and rolled away.

Menlo Park

He gave her the light bulb, the glass gone pink over the years. I can drop it? she said. He nodded, and she held her hand from the window, the traffic moving stories below.

Epistemology

He took her by the throat and squeezed. Motels, he said, they make me murder. She pushed him away and stepped onto the lawn. Lightning bugs lifted and fell, trucks on the highway busting the night. Shall we marry? she said, twirling her skirts. It was impossible to understand, the humid cloud of words.

A Millionaire's Time

He conceived of trucking a pillar into his backyard, but he wasn't sure what he'd do up there. He thought he might build something, a motorcycle, from bolts and rubber and carbon steel, or he thought he might burn, hot red through the day, cooling orange as the night decayed. He would pray, of course, the hair in his heart still there, the horrifying itch that kept him wringing his hands as a child, but he desired a human payment too, the sex of motorcycle, the pain of skin, the worship of TV. Poor mendicant, he told himself, imagining grand torture, the lust of a crippled messiah.

At Last

He chalked the walls, plumbing it square and blued. Finished, it was a spider making to the eye. They watched movies there, remembered themselves across the atlas of synapses.

The Willful Child

Her doctor told her it was the bite of a brown recluse, the dime-sized wound on her palm. She believed this, knowing that if there were a god, he'd come to her as a spider. Of course, she knew there wasn't, and as the wound deepened and went purple, her heart refused to give it blood. She lay gaping on the bathroom floor, her hand the look of dead roses, her body an excitement of shudders. Help me, she told her father through the telephone, I'm sorry for everything I've done.

As Light Becomes St. Paul

In 23 directions of gray, the girl puts her hand to the sharp building's edge, gathering together some long-standing anger. He watches her, the spirograph pigeons, waiting for the flush of blood to her throat that'll somehow be the signal for morning.

PITH

When he checked the door that last time, it was open, malice leaking free like dry heat. Yes? he called and rattled the ring of keys at his hip. No, came the answer, the voice not unlike his lover, his mother, a wounded horse.

Where The Woods Is Darkest

The filmmaker forgets his camera. He goes to the river instead, ice sliding by in blue sheets. On one is a man cooking over a pale fire. *Hey*, says the man, sliding by. *By the time this melts, I'll be in warmer parts.* The filmmaker sells his camera. He makes out for the desert, writing poems like sun under static.

Cartogram

The green cuts to tan—textures of a grocery bag—the rivers bluer, counties wider. They opened out, out there, thoughts losing the yellow gridwork of cities, marked with the spare periods of desert towns. You are here? she wrote, across the legend, waiting 5, 10, 100 miles for an answer.

Light Of No Understanding

He asked of her, Take this. She held it, turned it over, set it on her table.

Valentine

There seemed to be impossible things, crossing the sidewalk, adjusting the birds, the smoke from a concrete pipe. He had a valve that was wrong, perched whitely among the viscera. He tried small and smaller tries.

80

With 400 miles of farmland they seemed forever resting under one tree or another. They showed each other things from their pockets, pointed to the cows sleeping in the dust. Of it all, it was her small shirt he loved the most.

East-Eden

She worked equations—the body mass of athletes, ice skaters—her pencils blackening the pages. Through this, he dealt his cards. Hearts! he yelled, in the kitchen, to whichever neighbor or song might be playing.

The Love Of
The Lazabout's Wife

He watched the glaze of August from the steps, the dirty basketball boys and garbage trucks. Well? she said. What have you done? He could point to the dandelions he'd seen or the lakes he'd imagined, the hot cold water of want, but she would laugh and turn away. Didn't think so, she said. Still, there was more summer in her mouth than he would have known in a wild of work.

Eleven

As she read essays, she plaited one side of her hair. You'd last forever, he said, up from his puzzle. The green light of some vehicle tracked across the ceiling.

Exegesis

She sat flipping among his book, fingers glasslike on the pages. Funny then when she was cut, spattering blood on the girls' varsity squad. *Have a great summer!* it said, arrow inked up the center's skirt.

Diction

It was easy to hear the word that turned through the table. It could sound like *death*, or *listen!* or *ridicule*, but it caught at the throat and stuck. The other words, those at the spiked green corners of her eye or the bittersweet planes of his mouth, were pregnant with it, its sons and daughters. They'd labor on, these people, without fruit it seemed, though in fact the table was sweet in the blossoms of it.

A Brace Is Not a Couple

At the back of the store, beneath shelves of porcelain cats, were bags of confetti. Some look like guts, she said, and red spaghetti. He wouldn't make the obvious rhyme, though he saw through her eyes the rising birds.

St. Avia's Epistle

Wet pills of dirt at the grass's white radicle, the half-worm breathing consonance, eat me, find me, want me.

PIKE

The bridge was broken, just a causeway for squirrels, though underneath girls made promises to boys. She pointed them out, named them by their best feature—*hair* or *eyes* or *breasts*. A year ago, this time on open water, he'd named her too.

Absorbance

On the eraser board she wrote blood, crossed it out, wrote tears, pushed her hand through it, wrote lachrymal ducks. She turned to her students. They were already bored by her, her dry hysterics, except for a tiny Nepalese girl. Ma'am, said the girl, rising from her seat, about to cry out or laugh, her labshirt breast stained Coomassie blue.

Easter Rabbit

Can you save me? Yes. Put your head down. I'm afraid it'll hurt. It will. No one wants it.

Biography

There is a price. It's on the back. If you turn it around you'll see. It isn't expensive. Everything's okay.

The Gossipers

The red sweater of her sat with cups empty. Do you want him? said her friend. No, she answered. Just his voice. He, not so far away, spoke. In this way, they invented a machine, her gilt wheels, his explosions. It ran into the night, across several years. Friends regarded it with amusement and teeth. He sat with the red sweater of her. The sun beside you, he said. I know, she answered. Who would invent stories against them?

Loss

She burned the shirt in the backyard, the green smoke an ugly whiplash, the buttons popping.

I still don't get it, he said.

What? That I have one less shirt? The fire was pale, shining on her arms.

Ten Thousand Things

The man moved over the city like a small dog, heedful in scent and strikingly gray. With each step his palms signified old men and children, their stoops, held at the center level of circulation.

Parallax

She holds up a triangle she's made of polished wood. Like it? she says. He has to keep his hands from pulling apart its delicate joints, built in the far corner of her room, brought to bear in this crowd. No, he says, and they look at him, these people he has.

The Idealist

The lake drained to mud, the oars and barrels and cracked dinnerware drunken among the new weeds. If there's quicksand, she said, would you pull me out? He shook his head. I'd go down too. And then which of us would bear our future children? She laughed, already up to her knees.

TRESPASS

He took a glass of ice water into the women's bathroom.
She squatted next to the dirty bowl, sweat on her nose.
Please, she said, this stranger, this sick girl.

St. Sebastian's

His foot had ached for months, a slow stab, heartbroken pain. *There's nothing wrong with it*, said the doctor. The remorse of a red handkerchief stuck from his lab coat pocket. *Of course, that doesn't make it unreal.* He thanked the doctor and went to the park, the low bubble of children, the pale, beatific mothers.

INCORPORATED

His hands were covered in correction fluid, blotched white to the wrists. The man at the next desk watched over his computer screen, speaking slowly into the phone. With each jab of the brush, the photograph withdrew. Business proceeded.

Manifest

She crowded it, hawking its colors, lengths. *It's awful*, she said. *How bad it is is tragic.* It was a tower of cups and strings, motherboard, throat of a large bird. He stood in the ozone of her disgust. He took her mouth, kissed it, held it.

Maude Gonne Is A Bomb

She swam to the first sandbar and stood with the lake-waves at her knees. A boat with three boys idled by. He heard the word fish and skin and she laughed. She waved to him before turning out, arms angled for colder water.

On Not To See A Bird

The noodles boil to paste, blacken, catch fire. She comes home and throws the pot into the snow, a hissing startled crow. Upstairs, she finds him asleep, eyes clenched to the plumes of acrid smoke. She slides beside him, has dreams—acres of corn-stalk, winter rag—pinioned by the wing of his arm.

Fault

He saw her at the crumbled line of spring, the quaver-headed jonquil in their bed. She smelled of paperwhite and tan. They posted *Caution* to protect her beauty, signed the plot, the vows, the earth-moving machines.

Grand

The earth broke and they stood looking, the soaring backs of the crows. He thought he might drop a penny, have them carry it over the desert like a red egg. She thought she might drop herself, wind sliding up her skirt like a friend's hand.

THRIFT

Her face fresh from the barber was small and fragile, a bulb of milk ready to be broken. It's irresponsible, he said. You can't throw money after love. But the room was in her eyes and all the street outside.

Should They Offend

When she gave up speed and the sky turned back to blue, she realized most of all she needed things in her hands, stones she found in the street, a dog's tail, the legs of men. Forever she'd been tied to the eyes: Feed me or cut me off, said her hands, I am starved. Whatever she touched became clean.

A WISH

A pebble sank for 3 days through 3 miles of water. It passed between the skeleton of a whale, in which a school of orange fish lived. When it reached the bottom, it wouldn't move again, missing terribly the sailor's hand.

SET

Ever have one of these? she says. She's holding a green candy, hard and exquisitely square. No, he says, falling over and over and over.

Ascent

She stood weeping on the cement, behind her the million pounds of the city, the 10 thousand legs and lungs, before her a dirt field, broken blocks, a blue thistle nosed by a beautiful dog.

Interruption

Afterward, her eyes started sharding the light, the view from the front door a modern cathedral. That dog is 47 types of brown, she told her husband. His forehead broke into 21 worries, though perhaps he only studied the faultless ceiling.

Another Thing

40 hinges—Hospital, churchyard, window, the dock, the dock, a mile of cherry water.

Lease

The wall had 4 switches in some arrangement of off and on, a single light. Click! she said. From the dark, she laughed. Click! she said again, but there was just black, in some arrangement of silver.

Cradle

It was rock bared by rain. *Here*, she said, indicating a slot of the thinnest soil. *Do we sleep here?* The red valley, like the draft of her hip, startled him from below.

Argot

The mice fought in the ceiling, squealing in rage. *Sure it's not rats?* he said. She plodded through her novel. *Rats would sound like cats. Cats like elephants.* The rain in its waves seemed white and holy.

Cardinal

I've never been south, she said. They lived in Bloomington, the road the black row in soyfields of birds. *Only north. Or east or west.* Noon fixed dust like snow.

Hardly, Not At All

For a couple months he saved the dollar that came from the bottom of her purse. It did not smell of pencils and coins, it had not known her naked.

&1/4

Here, he said, setting a quarter on the back of her hand. The coin was aglow, having spent winter under the ice out front. She touched the ribbon of its hair, the tropic motto.

Occupation

She said, You look thin.
 To what question she addressed, he—his red sweater on the bright day—couldn't guess.

STORIES
AROUND
PEOPLE

An Event

Facebook lived in midtown, for there the people and windows shone like water. Though it would board the bus—1 day—and ride to the sea, where people said words like *sea* and where the city shone in the waves and the fish were sidewalks and windows.

Bolt

In the night, the house where *Octopus* lived burned to the ground, all the letters and poems a curled ash. The other books patted its shoulder and gave it roses and tea. It stood admiring the sky and thankful.

A Labor

You do not understand, *vacuum* said, it's never been like that between us. In its jar, it knew this, seized it.

More from STORIES AROUND PEOPLE

It was that day *Kansas* lost a tooth chewing corn. It smiled at the sun, gold and gold and gold.

Mercy Seat didn't know who its friends were, whether to eat red pills and fill its eyes with velvet night, or sit home and pray. It had a child it didn't know; blessed that fruit with silver hands.

Bullion came in the shape of an egg. It waited for the water, that spectral cousin of steam.

It was the one that came at the end, when the crowd went home. It filled the place of black-note *dot*.

Deep Falls

History Of Encaustic

Someone had burned a candle, the wax spattered on the cement, pills of it in the trickle of the river. She lifted her arms and shouted, *It's later than you think!* laughing at the echo. He watched her feet rise and fall, marking so little in the yellow silt.

Lapse

Her hand was small enough to thread the fence, touch the bug that held to the wall.

—, she whispered, as it fell. *What?* he asked. *What?* she answered. She turned her head, her neck a bracket for the dropping day.

Ark

The river swelled beneath the stone, covered his shoe. He followed at a distance, one print on the dirt, the shape of her watered in the moon.

The Long Daylight Night

The three walked up from the stone walls and trees, 4 AM. Their hands smelled like paper, water, bridges, glue. They said goodnight and stood there, jaws shining, teeth bright, going nowhere.

Synecdoche

She went back through the trees, calling her dog, the dump of tables and chairs. On the far bank, the train. *Here*, it called. He sat among a ring of blue mushrooms, face to the sun.

Radio Show

You're bleeding, she said. *I know*, he answered. *It was that broken cement.* The *Closed Road* sign made noise with the wind, a thrush in the pothole. *Need this?* she said. She held out her hand, a napkin, a small sketch of his ear.

Mineral

The mountain of salt picked up the headlight and cracked it to a thousand cubes. *Do they mine it?* he said. *From the ground?* She paid no attention, taking her pulse, blood pushing against the pressure of her thumb.

Ascension

How many animals, she said, *you think live in this woods? How much flesh?* They thought of the birds, the rats, the snakes, the deer, the thousand bugs piled over the ground, squeezed among the leaves.

Dramatis

The column fed the noise of the highway exchange, 50 feet above, to her ear. *What's it sound like?* he said. *Ants*, she answered. *Chewing a tunnel through porcelain.* She shrugged, the slow fission of the silent day.

Track

Around back, the women who mail porn smoked cigarettes, dropping ash into black puddles. They blinked and shuffled as she raised a hand. *Hey*, they said, the band of trees tipping near.

Tabula Rasa

A man cut into the rotted cement with a hunting knife—I WANT—gathered up his garbage bag and dirty coat and shuffled on. She put her finger to the empty space, closed her eyes.

Yellow

The water falling smelled of ammonia and copper, slick as grease. Trapped in an eddy, swinging toward the edge, the banana was fluorescent, a crescent of sun. He was close enough to hear the graze of her breath, trapped at the edge of inertia.

Truck

Along the gutter ran a black rat, feet in the fallen leaves.
As he reached to tell her, the still broke.

Moses

A baby lay asleep in its carrier, among weeds, the mother shaping letters and faces on the wall. He watched the sprayback drift, speckle the ailanthus red. *She has the legs of a soldier*, she said.

Disclose/Agape

She found a wire cage holding the skeleton of a bird. She brought it to the road and opened the wire door. On the cement, with the bones, she spelled a subtle word.

Red Crane

They stood in its lee as the snow paperwhited the sky. *It smells of honey*, she said. It did, the gearboxes and grease, the black iron hook. He thought he might climb its tower, look out, bird's eye, new white view.

Priest

Through the window they saw the palms, the oranges, a red cat sitting buddha on the floor. *It's just glass*, she said, meaning the difference between inside and out. He nodded, a cruiser trolling by, the redheaded cop.

Narcissus

A boy stood to his ankles as the water and weeds of plastic curled by. *He'll be dead of leukemia*, he said, regretting already her smile, the blade of her shoulder, the lily of her eye.

Overpass

The lips were gray, the skull shown through at the temple. They left it there, only reluctantly, mesmerized by the failing light.

End

They turned right, off the road, left the smell of the river, the miasma of history. They looked at their hands and forearms for dust and scars. *Well?* she said, down the long blue lens of his sight.

God Not Otherwise

First Certainty, Ailanthus Tree

It was the kind of city he might bear, the river, the beautiful sidewalks, the pregnant dogs. He'd watch the flies and in their wings find things like braided water. *See that tree*, said a boy. He followed the arm, up the trunk, to the crown. *Yes?* He waited, sharp for completion, the short ash of the sky.

Second Certainty, Physic

To begin with, there was the girl in the gold dress, the angle of her collarbone in the heat. There was the man in the red jumpsuit too, steady hands on the wheels and levers of things. Both were fixed, imprinted with light against the backdrop. He felt himself shimmer, knees unbuckle, the sun's neat sugarpill.

INTERLUDE

One
At 4, the crew forgot the shovels. None of them would notice. They'd eat dinner, nearly holding to their forks.

Two
The woman unlocked the glass door, the fragile moment she smelled books.

Three
They fought, the blood from her nose washing the boy's feet.

Third Certainty, Heartbreak

Under the stairs a bottle stood. It took the light of the afternoon and cooled it, green and powdered. He saw it through his parted feet, the red-cracked boards. It ignored him, hard beyond glass, still beyond touch.

Fourth Certainty, Right Time

He shared a cigarette with the dentist, who'd just pulled a tooth, the nurse from next door. *I have a man inside*, she said, *with a tumor in his eye*. They stopped, marked the quiet of the suffering train.

BIOS

CHRISTINE SAJECKI is an artist whose encaustic paintings frequently involve dialogue with literature and with writers, especially inspired by the open space and generosity towards the human experience found in Joseph Young's microfiction. Her paintings and animations have shown in many venues in the United States and Europe. She currently resides in Savannah, Georgia. Visit her website at *csajecki.com*

JOSEPH YOUNG lives in Baltimore, Maryland. His work has appeared in *Lamination Colony, FRiGG, wigleaf, Caketrain, Grey Sparrow, Mississippi Review Online, Exquisite Corpse*, and *Smokelong*. He has written on art for a variety of magazines and newspapers, and some of this writing can be found at *www.BaltimoreInterview.com*.

He is fond of collaboration and has created art exhibitions in concert with a number of visual artists. Visit his microfiction blog at *verysmalldogs.blogspot.com*.

5 Lines Baltimore

A warehouse slid into the street, shuffle of yellow brick beneath the stoplight, no cars, but in the stone a man's cane, a gull's blood.

From the rich wood of the coffined attic the bats decanted, circled the turrets, a mugger with one eye rolled on the sky.

He walked beside the red pole, deep cut, black line.

A box of toys blew over, rain whipped the porch rail, a boy skinny and wet fed his cat through the window screen.

The steps were white cakes, green roses of beer bottles and dead flowers, a woman feigning sleep on the sidewalk.